091693

Desimini, Lisa
I am running away today.

I AM RUNNING AWAY TODAY

I AM RUNNING AWAY TODAY

LISA DESIMINI

HYPERION BOOKS FOR CHILDREN

NEW YORK

Jessica Katz

FOR MY FRIENDS...

Andrew Goldstein

Printed in Singapore by Tien Wah Press (Pte) Ltd.
FIRST EDITION
1 3 5 7 9 10 8 6 4 2
Library of Congress Cataloging-in-Publication Data
Desimini, Lisa.
I am running away today / Lisa Desimini.
p. cm.
Summary: Having decided to run away from home for
a host of reasons, but most of all because his best
friend moved away, a cat changes his mind when he
discovers a new friend moving in next door.
ISBN (trade) 1-56282-120-2. — ISBN 1-56282-121-0 (library)
[1. Cats — Fiction.   2. Runaways — Fiction.]   I. Title.
PZ7.D4505Iam 1992 [E] — dc20 91-25341 CIP AC

The artwork for each picture is prepared
with layers of oil glazing on bristol paper.
This book is set in 24-point Antique Olive Light.

Marlene Shan

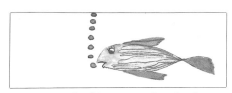

Natalie Desimini

Charlene Wetzel

Maureen Meehan

Katherine Murphy

Giavanna Bruno

Jerome Boxley

Frank Gargiulo

I am running away today.
My house is cold and creaky.

These trees are old and broken.
I've found their secret hiding places.

I've played with the same toys
day after day.

And now my best friend

just moved away.

So I'm off to look

for a new house.

I want a big house to play in,

but not too big. I might get lost.

It can't be too small
to stretch out my paws

or too tall
to climb to the roof
for a nap.

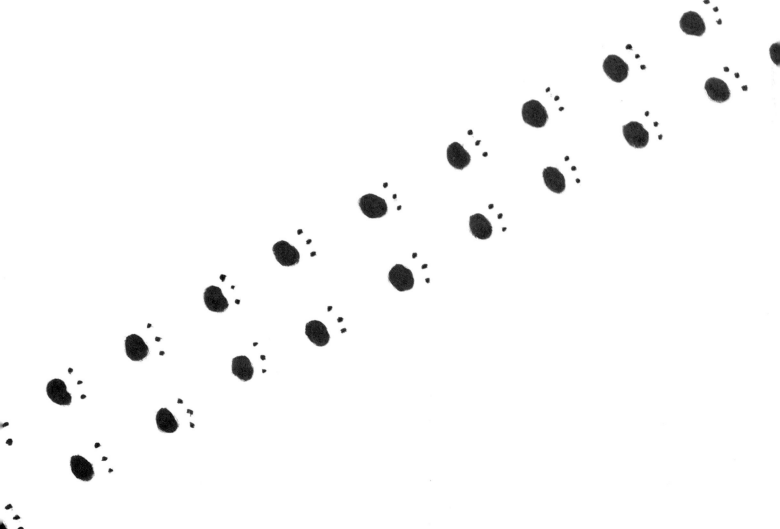

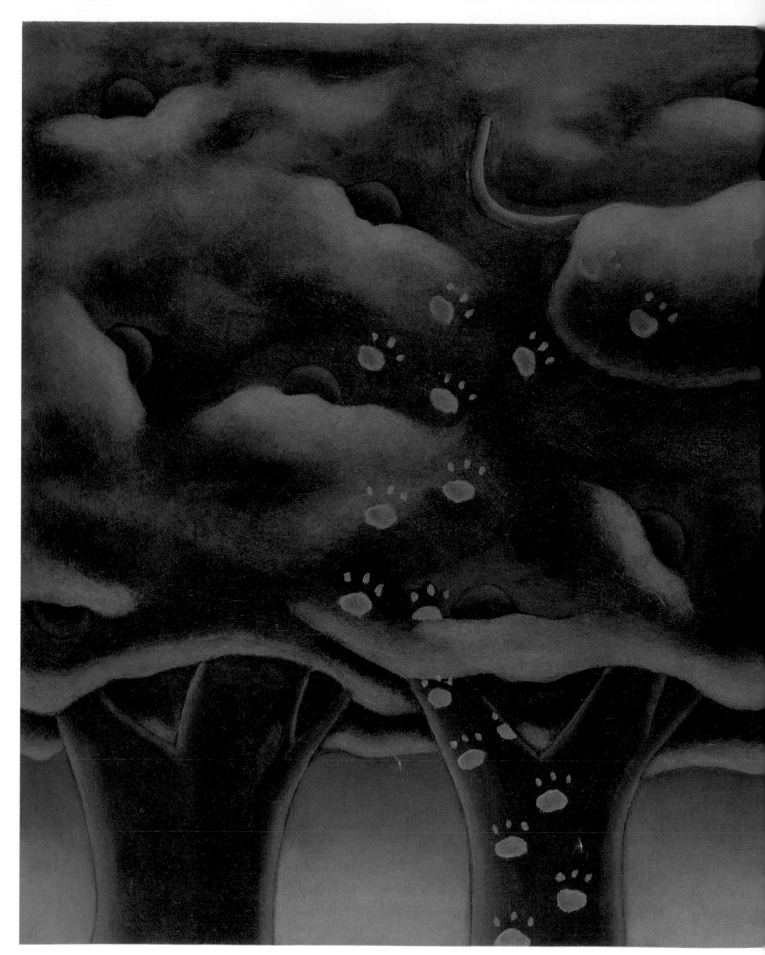

I need trees to

climb and hide in

and very big windows
so the sun can shine through.

With toys shaped like mice and cars
and fish that are blue.

My new house can be any color but pink—
pink doesn't match my coat.

At the top of that hill
is a crooked little house.
It's not too small or too tall.
It's cozy and bright,
the trees are just right,

and someone to play with

is moving in next door.

I think I'll stay.